A Friend for Noodles

Look for picture clues on page 26
to help you read this book.

Copyright © 2011 by Hans Wilhelm, Inc.

All rights reserved. Published by Scholastic Inc.
SCHOLASTIC, CARTWHEEL BOOKS, NOODLES, and associated logos
are trademarks and/or registered trademarks of Scholastic Inc.
Lexile is a registered trademark of MetaMetrics, Inc.

ISBN 978-0-545-34498-2

12 11 10 9 8 7 6 5 4 3 2 1   11 12 13 14 15 16/0

Printed in the U.S.A. 40 • First printing, September 2011

SCHOLASTIC READER
LEVEL 1
50-250 WORDS

A Friend for Noodles

by Hans Wilhelm

Cartwheel
·B·O·O·K·S·®

SCHOLASTIC INC.

New York   Toronto   London   Auckland
Sydney   Mexico City   New Delhi   Hong Kong

"I love fall!" says .

"There is so much to do!"

"Hello, !" says .
"Do you want to play?"
 runs after the .

He chases them around.

At last  catches the .

"Got you!" says .

Next wants to play with

his 🧸 .

Where is it?

"Someone stole my 🧸 !" says 🐕 .

 notices some fresh tracks.

They are not his tracks.

"I will find my ," says .

 follows the tracks into the woods.

They lead to a big, dark hole.
But  is not scared.

He wants his  back!
 creeps into the hole.
There is his !

And there is a small .

"You took my !" says .

The small  looks sad.

"I'm sorry," says the small .
 grabs his  and
runs away.

 brings his  home.

He is happy he found his .

But  is sad when he thinks

about the small .

"Maybe the  is lonely,"
says .

"That's why he took my ."

"I know what I'll do!" says .
 jumps up and runs back into
the woods.

creeps into the hole.

"Do you want to play hide-and-seek?"

he asks the small .

"Yes!" says the small .

The  smiles.

"Let's go!" says .

They run to a 🎃 patch.
🐕 hides behind a big 🎃.
The small 🦊 hides behind a small 🎃.

Hide-and-seek is fun.

But now  and the small

are hungry.

"I know where to go," says .

They run to an 🍎 tree.
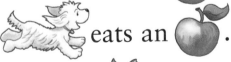 eats an 🍎.
The small 🦊 eats an 🍎.
They taste good!

"Look!" says . "A pile of !"
 and the  jump into
the .

"Yippee!"

The 🍁 dance in the wind.
🐕 and the small 🦊 love to
feel the wind blow.

"I love fall!" says the small .

"Me, too," says .

"Are you my friend?" asks the
small .
"Yes!" says . "I will even
share my  with you."

The small  smiles.

Then  and the small

roll down the hill all the way home.

There are six picture clues in this book. Did you spot them all?

Try reading the words on the following pages. If you need help, turn the page. The pictures on the other side will be your clue.

Reading is fun with Noodles!

Noodles

---

leaves

bear

---

fox

pumpkin

---

apple